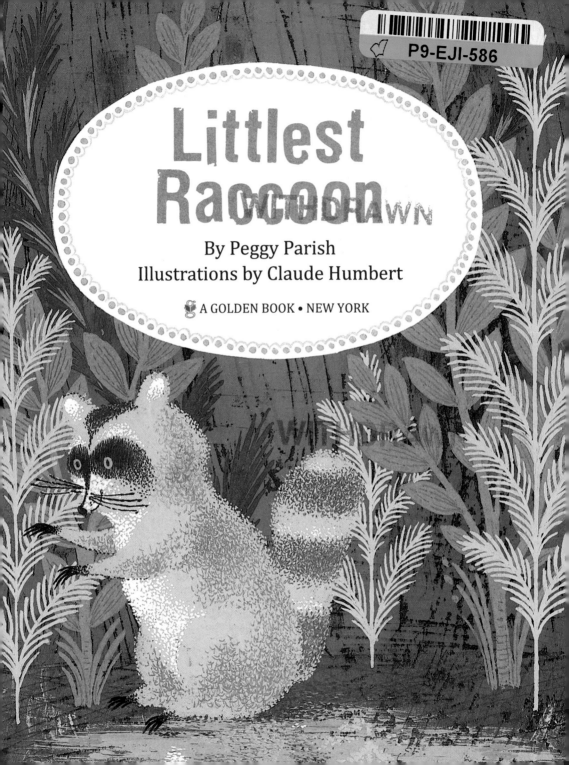

Littlest Raccoon

By Peggy Parish

Illustrations by Claude Humbert

A GOLDEN BOOK • NEW YORK

rhcbooks.com
Educators and librarians, for a variety of teaching tools, visit us at RHTeachersLibrarians.com
ISBN 978-0-593-38069-7 (trade) — ISBN 978-0-593-38070-3 (ebook)
Printed in the United States of America
10 9 8 7 6 5 4 3 2 1
2022 Edition

Deep in the forest is a tall tree. Gray Mouse lives in a little dark hole in its roots. Just above Gray Mouse, in a cozy hollow, lives Mrs. Raccoon.

Today Mrs. Raccoon is the proudest raccoon in the whole forest.

"Quiet," she says to Old Owl,
who lives in the next hole.
He just blinks sleepily.

"Quiet," she says to Woodpecker as he goes *peck, peck,* looking for insects to eat.

Then Mrs. Raccoon climbs back into her nest. She has three brand-new babies. Now she is Mother Raccoon. *That* is why she is so proud!

The babies are still tiny, and their brown coats are soft and fuzzy.

The babies nestle close to Mother Raccoon and they drink and drink. Such hungry baby raccoons!

Each day, the baby raccoons grow bigger. Soon Mother Raccoon decides to show them the world. Down the tree they go—Mother Raccoon and two baby raccoons. And last of all comes the littlest raccoon.

"This is grass," says Mother Raccoon.

The baby raccoons love the grass. They roll about and tumble in it. They play games in it. They even taste it!

Mother Raccoon watches proudly.

"These are my new babies," she tells Woodchuck. He nods politely and moves on. He is a busy woodchuck—much too busy to bother with baby raccoons.

"Time to go home," says Mother Raccoon.
Up the tree they go—two baby raccoons and
their mother. Where is Littlest Raccoon?

Mother Raccoon hurries down the tree to find her baby.

What has happened to him? Has that Wicked Fox stolen her baby? Wicked Fox is always hungry. And he likes raccoons most of all.

But no, Littlest Raccoon has just met Young Rabbit. They are playing Chase Me Round the Tree. Littlest Raccoon does not want to go home. He does not want to climb up that tall tree.

Mother Raccoon very firmly picks him up and takes him home.

One night, Mother Raccoon takes her children out
to look for food. Their eyes shine like little lights.

But soon Mother Raccoon sees only two pairs of
eyes. Uh-oh . . . Littlest Raccoon is gone again! Mother
Raccoon goes to look for her baby—quickly, before
Wicked Fox can get him!

Oh, there he is! He saw Prickly Porcupine and stopped to say hello. He wants to know why the porcupine has long, spiny needles instead of soft brown fur.

"Oh, what a worry you are, Littlest Raccoon!" says Mother crossly.

"This is water," says Mrs. Raccoon the next day.
"Nice fat fish live here."
    She reaches down to catch a big one.
    Littlest Raccoon gets so excited, he leans over
for a closer look. But oh, his foot slips, and—

SPLASH! Into the water he goes. No fish for anybody now. All the fish swim away. Mother Raccoon and two little raccoons shake their heads. Naughty Littlest Raccoon! Why is he always doing the wrong thing?

Green Frog is watching. "Too bad, Littlest Raccoon—too bad," he croaks.

Mother Raccoon is taking a nap in the sun.
The baby raccoons have gone to the apple tree.
Mother Raccoon taught them to listen for danger.
They will scoot to the tip-top of the tree if they
hear anything.

Littlest Raccoon and his big brother want the same red apple. Those little raccoons growl at each other. Then they scuffle around, and—the apple falls to the ground and rolls away.

"It's your fault, Littlest Raccoon," his big brother says crossly. Littlest Raccoon sighs.

The baby raccoons start back to their tree.

Oh, no! Look what they see.

Mother Raccoon is still sleeping—and there is Wicked Fox, coming up the path.

How frightened the baby raccoons are! Littlest Raccoon thinks quickly. This time, he must do the right thing.

And he does!
He runs to get help.
"Hurry, hurry," he tells his slow-moving friend,
Prickly Porcupine.

Wicked Fox is about to pounce on Mother
Raccoon. Instead, he leaps into the air—and runs
away, crying loudly.

Two little raccoons run to their mother. Where is Littlest Raccoon? Did Wicked Fox take him away?

No, there he is, with Prickly Porcupine. Oh, clever Littlest Raccoon! He knew just what to do to save Mother Raccoon from Wicked Fox. He went to find his friend Prickly Porcupine.

How proud Mother Raccoon is.
How proud his brothers are.
But proudest of all is Littlest Raccoon.
At last he has done just the right thing.